Disney fairies

Tinker Bell

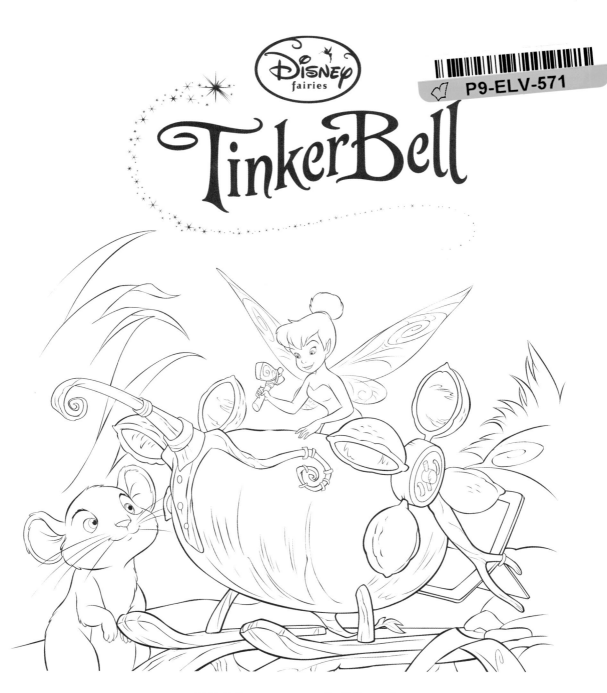

Flitterific!

Illustrated by the Disney Storybook Artists

A GOLDEN BOOK • NEW YORK

Copyright © 2010 Disney Enterprises, Inc. All rights reserved.
Published in the United States by Golden Books, an imprint of Random House Children's Books,
a division of Random House, Inc., 1745 Broadway, New York, NY 10019, and in Canada
by Random House of Canada Limited, Toronto, in conjunction with Disney Enterprises, Inc.
Golden Books, A Golden Book, and the G colophon are registered trademarks of Random House, Inc.
ISBN: 978-0-7364-2653-4
www.randomhouse.com/kids
MANUFACTURED IN MALAYSIA
10 9 8 7 6 5 4 3 2

A new fairy has arrived in Pixie Hollow.

"These things will help you find your talent,"
explains Queen Clarion.

The hammer glows and flies into the new fairy's hands. She is a tinker—Tinker Bell!

Rosetta is a garden fairy.

Color the flowers that contain the letters in Rosetta's name.

Iridessa is a light fairy.

Silvermist is a water fairy.

Use the key below to color the beautiful rainbow
Iridessa and Silvermist have created.

1 = Red   5 = Blue

2 = Orange   6 = Dark Purple

3 = Yellow   7 = Light Purple

4 = Green

1

2

3

4

5

6

7

Fawn is an animal fairy.

Clank and Bobble are tinker fairies, too. They show
Tinker Bell the way to her new home.

With a little snip here and there, Tinker Bell
makes her new clothes fit perfectly.

Tinker Bell meets Fairy Mary. She is in charge
of all the tinker fairies.

Vidia is a fast-flying fairy. "Fairies of every talent depend on me," she tells Tinker Bell.

Tink wants to learn a new talent.
But holding water droplets is hard!

Fawn shows Tink how to teach a baby bird to fly.

Draw a line from each bird to its match.

The bird is too scared to leave its nest.

Watch out for the hawk!

Tink is best at tinkering!

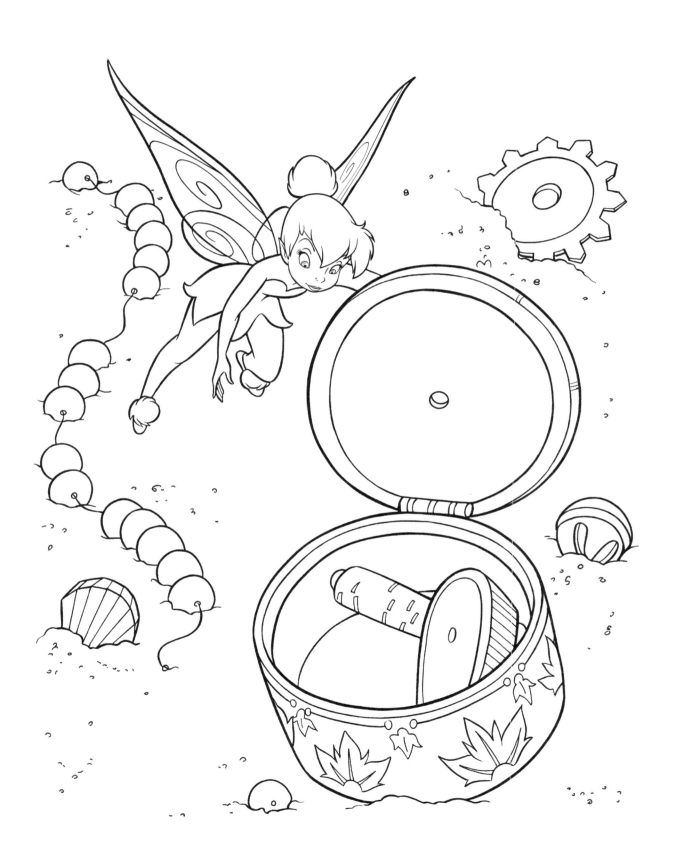

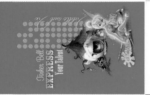    

Tinker Bell fixes a beautiful music box.
Connect the dots so the music can play.

The Minister of Spring is concerned that the fairies will have to cancel the changing of the seasons.

Tinker Bell has an idea! She gets right to work.

Tink's friends lend a helping hand.

Tink shows everyone how her inventions
can save spring.

Fairy Mary tells Tink she can go to the mainland to find the owner of the music box.

Tink's good friend Terence gives her some extra pixie dust for her trip.

Tink sprinkles the music box with pixie dust.

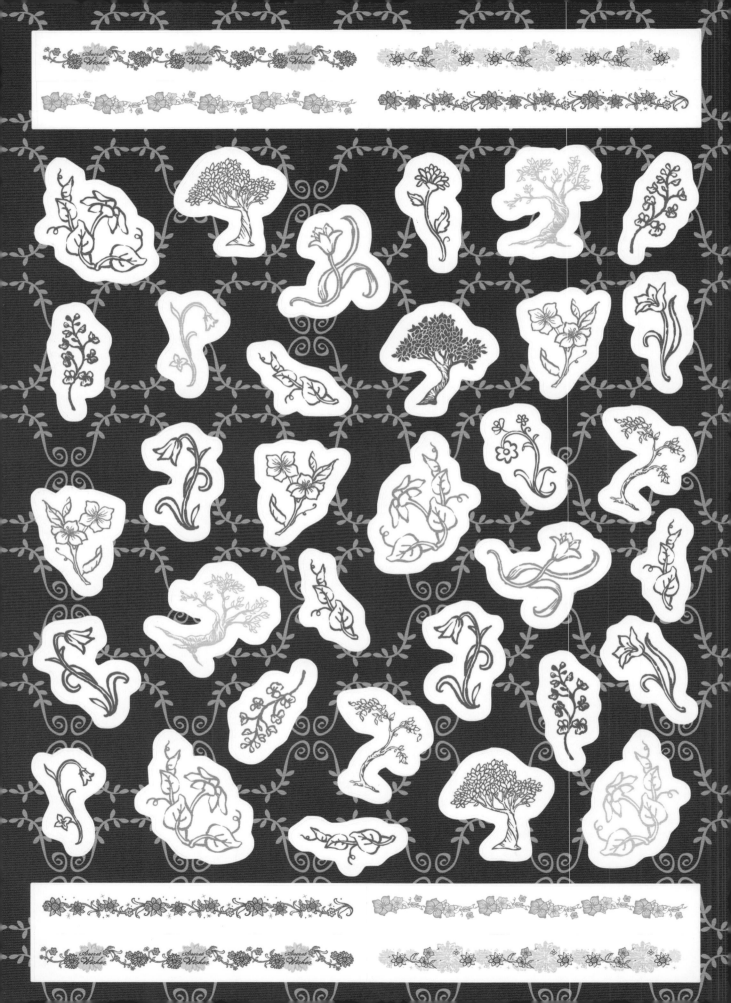

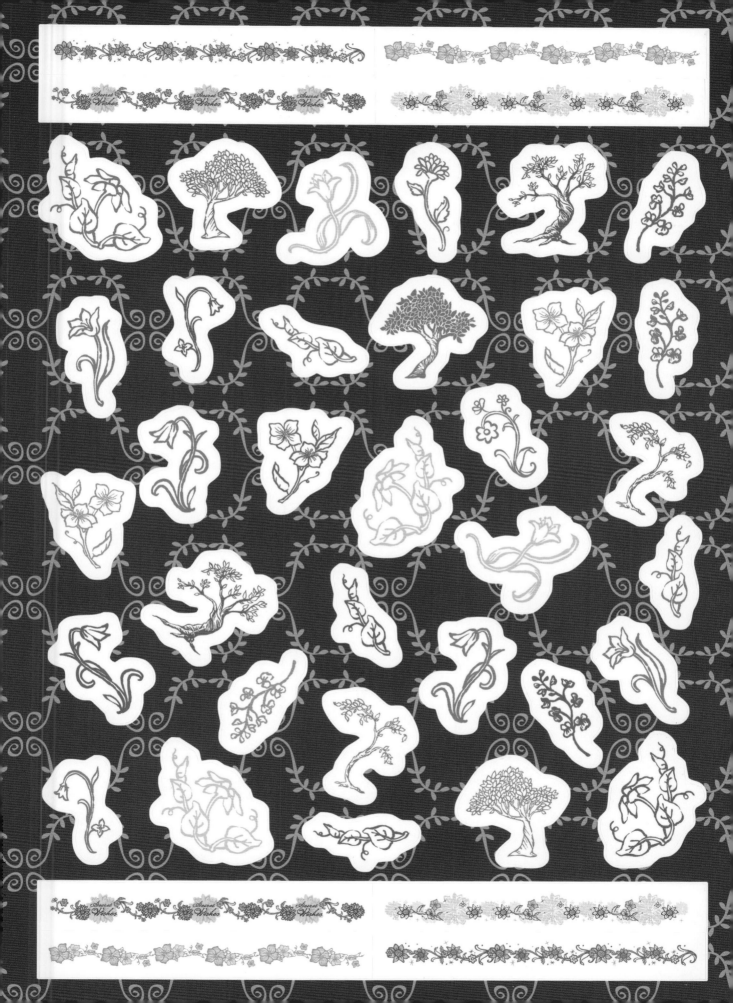

What an exciting journey!

Tink is working on a new invention.

Terence is always there to help Tink.

Tinker Bell is chosen to make the scepter
for the Autumn Revelry.

Fairy Mary gives Tinker Bell the beautiful moonstone.

Tink gets started right away.
This will be the best scepter ever!

Oh, no! The scepter is smashed!

And the moonstone shatters!
What will Tink do now?

It's the best Autumn Revelry ever—thanks
to Tinker Bell, Terence, and Blaze!

Look up, down, forward, backward, and diagonally to find all the names.

FAWN

IRIDESSA

BLAZE

TERENCE

ROSETTA

TINKER BELL

SILVERMIST

A Z E B T K T A
T S I L E E T P
S L S A R T I F
I R I E E S N A
M W N S D V K W
R C O Z V I E P
E R T I N E R S
V W F A W N B I
L A Z E V E E M
I F L E Z A L B
S K R O S T L A